The Castaways of Mar-a-Lago

An Absurdity Drama Novelette

James Musgrave

DEDICATION

This Absurdist drama is dedicated to all those great artists who came before me: Bunuel, Camus, Sartre (to some extent), Brecht, Calvino, Pynchon and Saramago, to name a few. Here's hoping there's a new renaissance of this rewarding and specialized form of literature.

INTERACTIVE AND MULTIMEDIA ENHANCED EBOOKS

EMRE Publishing is now selling completely "enhanced" versions of its books through the unique Embellisher Multimedia Stream platform. Simply register inside the eReader to have access to the variety of titles. They contain relevant historical videos, music, interactive content, and a complete audiobook edition in many of the great titles.

Visit https://emrepublishing.com/new_embellisher-ereader/ to see what's available. Enter your email and a password to register and view. Buy your future digital copies of Portia of the Pacific Historical Mystery series at reduced prices here:
https://books.bookfunnel.com/portiaofpacific

ACKNOWLEDGMENTS

I was watching the classic film by Luis Bunuel, *The Exterminating Angel,* and President Donald Trump and his administration had just entered office. It was 2016. I made the absurd connection between historical reality, and this drama by Bunuel, and connected it to my own life. The result is *The Castaways of Mar-a-Lago.*

Contents

CHARACTERS

Donald J. Trump and Melania
Ivanka Trump-Kushner and Jared Kushner
Sean Spicer and Rebecca Miller
Rex Tillerson (State) and Renda St. Clair
Mike Pence and Karen Pence
Rick Perry (Energy) Anita Thigpen Perry
Jeff Sessions (Attorney General) Mary Blackshear Sessions
Steven Mnuchin (Treasury) Fiancée Louise Linton
James Mattis (Defense General, USMC ret.)
Ben Carson (Housing and Urban Development) Candy Carson
Betsy DeVos (Education) Richard "Dick" DeVos (Amway)
Reince Priebus (Chief of Staff) and Sally Priebus
Stephen K. Bannon (Chief Strategist)
Tom Price (Health and Human Services) Betty Price
Kellyanne Conway (Counselor to President) George T. Conway III
Xi Jinping (President of People's Republic of China) and Peng Liyuan
Wang Liu Wei and Wang Li Chao (Secretaries to the President and his wife)
32 total in dinner party

PREFACE

The following is a transcription of what occurred during the Month of February, 2017, at the Mar-a-Lago Club on Southern Boulevard, Palm Beach, Florida. The narrator, one Nick Holcomb of Fox News, was the only reporter allowed to attend the dinner party held at a private event in honor of President Xi Jinping and his wife, Peng Liyuan. The President of the People's Republic of China had returned to America to attend a special showing of *Hamilton*, the musical being shown at the Palm Beach Kravis Center for the Performing Arts. Mr. Holcomb was allowed to use his voice recorder only, and no dialogues of a classified nature were to be recorded or discussed, since this was, in fact, a State Dinner paid for by U. S. Taxpayers. The United States Department of Homeland Security has expunged all portions of this recording that are considered classified information. The *National Enquirer* acquired this recording from Mr. Holcomb's upload while he was attending the memorial church services at the West Palm Beach Episcopal Church-by-the-Sea. He was able to edit it while the services were going on. It describes the strange events that took place inside Mar-a-Lago and, later, at the memorial service in West Palm Beach. We hope it may help to assuage the street violence taking place in America and in China at this time. There have been many rumors that allege various plots by the Russians and terrorist organizations, including ISIS, and we hope you can see from this recording that there was no subterfuge or violent overthrow such as took place, for example, in Turkey. No, Mr. Holcomb's audio recording speaks for itself, and we leave it to the people to judge for themselves about what happened.

CHAPTER ONE: THE GATHERING

This is a real break-out opportunity for me. As a recent graduate of the University of Florida, I'm going to attend the musical play *Hamilton* and then a sponsored dinner party in honor of the President of the People's Republic of China. Since we've been having some public relations problems with our owner and top opinion reporter here at Fox News, I was told to keep a very low profile and just become the proverbial "fly on the wall" at this event. That means I am not to give my own opinion about anything that I hear or see. I would hardly jeopardize my first big chance at Fox by making an ass of myself.

Unless, of course, I could get more money and a better career advancement somewhere else. The *National Enquirer* has just given me an offer I cannot refuse, and I now have free reign to report what I want to report, no matter how infamous or gossipy, and no matter how injurious to the Trump Administration it might prove to be.

The *Hamilton* musical presented at the Kravis Center featured all the cast from the original New York Broadway version, and it was stupendous! I am now driving out to Mar-a-Lago from the theater, with many of the songs from the hip-hop musical gushing out of my speakers. For some reason, I identify most with the Aaron Burr character. The song "Wait For It" was especially mesmerizing.

I see President Trump as if I were Aaron Burr, even though it's obvious I'm just a lowly journalist. He is a man of opinion and action, like Alexander Hamilton, and I am an observer of life, as this was why I was attracted to journalism in the first place. But men like Mr. Trump fascinate me, and I plan to watch and listen to him carefully as he and his beautiful wife, Melania, host this dinner party with all of these government officials attending. There will be fifteen high-ranking members of President Trump's inner sanctum at this gathering in honor of President Xi Jinping of China. I plan to describe all of what happens to the *National Enquirer*, whether it's good, bad, or ugly.

As I drive around the last bend in South Ocean Boulevard, I imagine what it might have been like for Marjorie Merriweather Post, the original owner of Mar-a-Lago, as she came upon the 17 ocean-to-lake acres leading up to the main club house on that 1927 winter season opening of her estate.

Mrs. Post was the heiress to the General Foods cereal fortune, and her daughter, actress Dina Merrill, is said to be worth over five billion dollars today, at age 93. She was raised inside this mansion, and I can imagine her as a version of F. Scott Fitzgerald's Daisy Buchanan, she with the "name that is full of money."

My great-grandmother, Gladys McKenzie, was the head housekeeper of the late "Mr. Palm Beach," Charles Munn, the owner of the patents to the pari-mutuel betting computer and the mechanical rabbits that greyhounds race to catch. His mansion, Amado, was located next-door to the winter home of the famous Joseph and Rose Kennedy family.

My mother, Mandy McKenzie-Holcomb, told me about her grandmother while she was working as a nurse to put me through college. We had little money, so the descriptions of all the affluence at the residence in Palm Beach were fascinating to me. All I had ever known were apartments in Miami, both military and civilian, as my father had been a Florida National Guardsman who died during his third deployment to Afghanistan.

Mother said her grandmother was an alcoholic who had a child out of wedlock after the Second World War. That was my grandmother, Jean Elizabeth McKenzie. The Munn family paid for my great-grandmother's funeral, and our family's only connection to the rich was the death bed secret my great-grandmother whispered to my grandmother. My Grandma Jean confessed this secret to my mother, Mandy, and then my mother told me: the man who was Grandma Jean's father was a Jew. Not only that, but when my mother first saw a picture of Jared Kushner, our president's current son-in-law, she exclaimed, "That's him! That's the man who was your Grandma Jean's father!"

Of course, that was impossible, but when my mother showed me the photo, I was amazed. Yossel (Joseph) Kushner, Jared's grandfather, was a holocaust survivor who, when photographed in 1949 in New York City, looked almost exactly like his grandson, Jared. My great-grandmother had shown this 1949 photo to my grandmother while on her deathbed, and my mother had shown it to me when she told me this family secret. Yossel was a married man whose wife, Rae, was also a survivor who had tunneled out of the Polish town of Novogrudek into the forest in 1943. They made a movie about this armed group of Jews fighting the Nazis in the forest, and it was called *Defiance*.

Charles, Jared's father, was the son of my great-grandfather Yossel. Charles was a real estate man like his friend, Donald Trump, but Charles was convicted by a jury in 2005 of 18 counts of tax evasion, making illegal campaign contributions, and witness tampering. And now his son Jared is married to President Trump's daughter, Ivanka. Of course, if I explained to Jared Kushner how he was related to me and my mother, he would probably think I was crazy.

My family was never admitted into the Kushner dynasty because my great-grandmother was not wealthy and she was not a Jew. She was simply an attractive Irish woman who was viewed as a temptation but who could never be accepted as an equal. In America, servants who reside with the wealthy are castaways on islands of excessive privilege based on birthright and upon generations of legal maneuvering in order to keep this wealth inside the family.

I suppose the only other person besides me at this gathering who doesn't care much for the Kushner family would be Stephen Bannon. He is known as an anti-Semite who once had an argument with his then wife Mary Louise Piccard about sending their twin daughters to a private school in Los Angeles. It came out during divorce proceedings that Mr. Bannon had once grabbed her by the throat and told her he didn't want his daughters going to school with Jews.

I have always found it intriguing that the wealthy folks in America quite often make their fortunes in real estate and from the so-called "sin products" of Wall Street gambling, alcohol, tobacco and other addictive drugs. Of course, Marx and Engels wrote about the evils of owning property in their *Communist Manifesto,* and the Kennedy family made a fortune from whiskey during Prohibition.

And, most of the rich gamble on Wall Street. In fact, Mr. Trump was only able to charge $100,000 to Mar-a-Lago members because many of them had been swindled by the Ponzi scheme of Bernie Madoff, and they couldn't afford more.

Both Stephen Bannon and the Treasury Secretary, Steven Mnuchin, made fortunes working for one of the main perpetrators of the Mortgage Crisis of 2008, Goldman Sachs. However, the two men then moved into the media business; Bannon to Breitbart News and Mnuchin to Hollywood, where the Russian Jew produced such popular films as *Avatar.* Bannon has not remarried, but Mnuchin is bringing his fiancée, a young Scottish actress, Louise Linton, to this dinner. She made a couple of low-budget movie thrillers that weren't well received.

I'm going to keep a close eye on Bannon and the two Jews, my secret cousin Jared Kushner and Steve Mnuchin, the Hollywood munchkin. Many alt-right supporters of Bannon want Kushner demoted from his lofty White House chief adviser position. When Bannon was taken out of the president's inner circle, the anti-Semitism on the Internet reached a fever pitch.

I believe what my Grandma Jean always said about the rich. All you need to do is follow the trail of money to see who's being dishonest, and it rarely, if ever, has to do with religion or ethnic heritage. It has most to do with selfish greed and with the exploitation of the lower classes.

I also find it strange that most of Trump's inner circle made their money from the investment bankers of Wall Street, and then, once they got some distance from the true source of their wealth, they began speaking out the other sides of their mouths about the conspiracy of the Globalists and the Elite Corporatists who take jobs away from Americans. Bannon and his alt-right followers are now fighting Kushner, Mnuchin and the other members of Trump's stable of right-wing Jews.

However, they are Jews, and because of the anti-Semitic ideas which blame the Worldwide Jewish bankers and other elites, Breitbart followers often talk about how America went to war for the Jews in Iraq and Afghanistan, and now they again accuse the Jews of forcing Trump to get involved militarily in Syria.

Again, it becomes a matter of being accepted into the inner circle and not becoming a castaway. Sadly, most of America, like me, is now in the role of an observing castaway, watching this absurd political drama play itself out in places like Mar-a-Lago.

The main house here at Mar-a-Lago is an adaptation of the Hispano-Moresque style, long popular among the villas of the Mediterranean. It is crescent-shaped with an upper and lower cloister along the concave side of the building that faces Lake Worth. A seventy-five foot tower tops the structure, rendering a magnificent 360 degrees view. That's another thing about the rich. They really like towers and walls.

Donald John Trump and his then wife, Ivana, bought Mar-a-Lago from the Post estate in 1985, for ten million dollars. The Post Estate had granted the property to the U. S. Government for use as a winter White House. However, the government said it was too costly to keep, and the security problem of being in Palm Beach International's flight path was too much of a risk.

Therefore, after Trump won a battle with the City of Palm Beach, he opened Mar-a-Lago as a private country club in 1995, charging folks $100,000 to join and $14,000 a year dues. Now that he's the President, Mr. Trump charges them $200,000 to join his club.

I guess the only battle Trump has with the city today, as I drive into the clubhouse entrance, is about the gigantic American flag he has waving on the grounds. As it happens, Trump's flag is larger than what the city permits. Trump has a problem with the size of something? Nah, I can't believe it!

As I park my little Prius and walk up to the rear servants' entrance, I overhear a conversation between the Maître d'hotel and one of the other dining room servants.

"Lorenzo, where are you going?" the Maître d' asks.

"I'm going for a walk," the servant replies.

"We have over thirty important guests arriving in an hour. Go back inside at once!"

"I'm sorry, Pedro, but I have to leave."

"If you leave, Lorenzo, you will never set foot inside Mar-a-Lago again!"

Lorenzo looks frantically around, as if he is being pursued, and he darts out into the parking lot. He then starts to run at full speed without looking back.

The Maître d'hotel swivels on his polished black shoes and grabs the golden handle of the elegant mahogany wooden door with gold inlay. He holds it open and motions for me to enter, glancing at the press pass that is affixed to my tuxedo jacket as I pass by him.

He's a tall man of Hispanic origins, and he is wearing an abbreviated tuxedo so as to differentiate himself from the more distinguished guests. His anguished demeanor makes his dark face look furtive, as he glances all around, looking for something out of order or for someone who's not where he or she is supposed to be.

"Come with me, Mister?" He asks, as he steps out in front of me

"Holcomb. But you can call me Nick," I tell him, as we stride into the magnificent confines of the carpeted dining room.

Several banquet room attendants are setting gold plates at the 34 places of the marble-topped, 30 by 50 feet table that weighs 4,000 pounds. The walls are covered with Sixth Century Flemish nature murals, and marble columns support the vaulted, 30-foot high, gold-inlaid ceiling.

"This room was built to resemble Rome's Chigi Palace, which was used as an office for Mussolini. Thus, we have the beautiful fresco wall paintings. Aren't they sublime?" Pedro waves his hand at the scene as he walks in front of me.

"It's quite impressive," I say, watching the staff carefully lay out the silver for formal dining. Two sets of spoons, knives and forks, as well as linen napkins with the Trump "T" embroidered in gold on their fronts. They are also laying out sets of chopsticks.

"Did anybody argue with Lorenzo about anything?" Pedro asks.

"No, he was saying how he would need help escorting the guests to their places. When he left, I didn't know where he was off to." A tall waiter says.

"Well, if he doesn't like it here then good riddance. There are plenty more across the border who want his job," says Pedro.

"I thought President Trump was against hiring illegals," I say.

"They aren't illegal," Pedro smiles. "All *el jefe* wants is the correct paperwork, *es verdad, mi amigos?*"

I overhear a short waiter next to me whisper in a snickering tone, "You got the money, we get you the green card, *amigo*." He grabs the Maître d' by his sleeve. "Hey Pedro. You seen that movie called *A Day Without a Mexican?*"

"I keep telling you, Arturo. I don't watch political propaganda. You get a job and you keep it. There is no politics involved in that." Pedro takes my arm and guides me into the kitchen.

"It was funny, man. The government thinking we're aliens from outer space 'cause we disappear!" Arturo tells us as we pass him.

Three kitchen workers and the main cook, a woman, are putting the evening's meal together. In honor of the Chinese head of state, there is Peking roast duck, egg foo yung, what looks to be six different rice dishes, and a huge Mandarin orange salad.

"We're having President Trump's favorite dessert, however, German chocolate cake," says Pedro. "Have you made the cakes yet, Alicia?" He asks the cook.

"Yes, they're made. We all need to leave soon, before they come," says Alicia.

"Leaving? What if the guests need something extra?" Pedro's voice sounds frantic.

"I don't care. You take care of them," says Alicia, and the others nod in agreement with her.

"What's happening around here? First Lorenzo and now you. Do you all want to get banished from Mar-a-Lago?"

A young man sticks his head inside the kitchen. "They're here! The cars are pulling up out front!"

"Oh, my God!" Pedro yells, and he sprints out of the kitchen.

"Let's go! We have to get out of here," says Alicia, throwing down her apron. The other workers follow her out of the kitchen, and I decide to follow them.

We all take the kitchen freight elevator down to the lobby floor. When we exit, the guests are just entering the club's portico entrance, and there is nobody to take their coats and guide them into the dining room. That had been Lorenzo's job.

Obviously not wanting to be seen by the dignitaries, Alicia, the other kitchen staff, and I duck back into the elevator and watch the officials climb upstairs to the dining room on their own.

When the last person disappears, Alicia again opens the door to the freight elevator and pokes her head out. There is, once again, a group of people who are entering the lobby. I swear to God, they are the exact same persons we saw just moments before!

However, as if they were used to this kind of mysterious event happening every day, Alicia the cook and her entourage quietly wait inside the elevator until this second group has made its way up the stairs to the dining room made in the image of the Chigi Palace. I wonder what the second identical group will say to the first group when they meet them upstairs?

I feel like leaving this rather haunted mansion along with Alicia and the kitchen help, but I decide to find out what the real answer is that might explain what I'm experiencing. I haven't smoked weed since college, so it can't be that. I haven't had anything to eat or drink, so it can't be a drug that I've been given.

Maybe it's the way the staff is acting. Is there going to be a terrorist bombing? Perhaps one of those groups is a decoy, you know, the way Josef Stalin and Saddam Hussein were said to have had doubles made of them to trick assassins.

I exit the freight elevator and go upstairs, expecting at any moment to be jumped by CIA agents, terrorists, or both. However, all I can see are the photos of the smiling Trump family all along the walls leading up to the dining room. I can smell the food, and I can hear the rumble of conversation coming from the room.

CHAPTER TWO: THE DINNER

None of the hotel staff is here, and when I open the door to the dining room, I immediately hear the unmistakable voice of Donald J. Trump, the leader of the most powerful country in the world.

"Folks, we're not going to be bothered by the Secret Service or any other bodyguards. Also, we're not allowing club members to see the nuclear football and tweet it to their friends. This is Mar-a-Lago, a club that has represented freedom from oppression starting the moment it first came into being, but we must now protect Mar-a-Lago from prying eyes, even if it means keeping out the Secret Service, most of the media, and even private club members. I won the battle with the City of Palm Beach. No more international airport traffic noise flying overhead since I became President! We still have our drones in the sky, and our military guardians are right outside to keep us safe inside. Besides, I see President Xi is wearing his military uniform this time, so we'll let him protect us. How about that, Mr. President? But you'll have to crank it up a notch if you want to catch up to America's defense weapons, right Mad Dog?"

President Trump looks out over the seated dignitaries to an older man with a gray, USMC buzz-cut, sitting at the far end of the table, who appears to be quite uncomfortable in his black tuxedo. He looks like an old bloodhound who doesn't hunt anymore. "Mr. President, please I told you, I don't want to be called that name anymore. It doesn't go with the dignity of my office."

"Sorry, James. I know. But that name sounds so very bad-ass."

There are several chuckles that erupt from the men seated around the long table.

Secretary of Defense James Mattis is the only bachelor here besides Mnuchin and Bannon, but the former Marine Corps "mustang" General is a confirmed bachelor, and he was never married to any partner other than the military. A mustang is an officer who was once an enlisted man, and, as a result, he usually has a soft spot in his heart for the enlisted soldiers under him.

Mattis is certainly well loved by his troops. My father always told me these mustang officers are usually not chicken-shit about inspections and all the other formalities of the military. They care only about what counts: whether you survive on the field of battle.

My old friend Pedro rushes up to me as I stand inside the door watching everything. "Mister Holcomb? Let me show you where you're sitting. I'm sorry, but we seem to be experiencing a strange depletion of staff. Mrs. Trump and I are looking into it."

I am seated next to Steven Mnuchin's fiancée, the actress, Louise Linton.

The wives and husbands have been placed across from each other so as to break-up the sexes for conversational purposes. Obviously, there is no second group of guests. I want to tell somebody about what I saw, but I decide to keep it to myself for the time being.

The seating is arranged around me, in the following order, to my right, around the table: Louise Linton, Sean Spicer (Press Secretary), Rex Tillerson (Secretary of State), James Mattis (Defense), Anita Thigpen Perry (Rick Perry's wife), Dick DeVos, Stephen Bannon, Kellyanne Conway (President's Counsel), Renda St. Clair (Rex Tillerson's wife), Jeff Sessions (Attorney General), Jared Kushner (President's Senior Adviser), Rebecca Miller (Sean Spicer's wife), Dr. Ben Carson (Secretary of Housing and Urban Development), Betsy DeVos (Secretary of Education), Reince Priebus (President's Chief of Staff), Dr. Tom Price (Secretary of Health and Human Services), Donald J. Trump (President of United States), Xi Jinping (President of China), Wang Li Chang (Female Personal Secretary to Peng Liyuan, Jinping's wife), Steven Mnuchin (Secretary of the Treasury), Karen Pence (Vice President Pence's wife), Ivanka Trump-Kushner, George T. Conway III (Kellyanne's husband), Candy Carson (Ben Carson's wife), Melania Trump (First Lady), Mary Blackshear Sessions (Jeff Session's wife), Mike Pence (Vice President), Betty Price (Tom Price's wife), Wang Liu Wei (Male Personal Secretary to President Xi Jinping), and Peng Liyuan (President Xi Jinping's wife).

So, there are 33 total guests in this dinner party, including yours truly.

"Excuse me. Are you recording?" Louise Linton asks me, and I turn toward her.

She is, by far, the most attractive woman at the table. Why not? She's an actress. Blonde hair is rolled into a tousled top-knot bun, her white formal dress looks like it's made of chiffon or some other delicate cloth, and her face has what I like to call a "perpetual look of Hollywood innocence," which current and wannabe stars wear in order to contrast with all the sexy roles they must play on the screen. Her Scottish accent is also quite alluring.

Of course, she's listening to me as I'm saying this, and she smiles. "I was an undergrad Journalism major at Pepperdine. I like your style. You can always go over this recording later and polish it, right? I wish they'd done that with the thrillers I was in. In Hollywood, low budget means not much editing work. Editing that's as flimsy as my batiste gown. You see, it's often best to ask the primary source about facts like wardrobe. That look of innocence can also get you out of drug busts."

"I think I'll do more recording of this distinguished gathering and keep my mouth shut. Remember when journalism used to be all about the story and not about the celebrity journalist? When you compare Edward R. Murrow with Bill O'Reilly, you can see what I mean. Murrow said we'd lose our objectivity because of the race for high ratings, and I guess he was right.

I've gone from working at Fox News to the *National Enquirer*. I, Nick Holcomb, have gone from the proverbial frying pan into the fire."

"Well, now that I'll be married to one of the biggest and most successful producers in Hollywood, I believe my roles will be improving also. Good luck, Nick Holcomb, on your own upgrade. Enjoy the meal!"

President Trump speaks from the head of the table. "We are here to pay our respects to the two greatest nations in the world. Despite the little guy in North Korea, I believe we can do business together to keep the world safe and profitable. I must say that my wall is going to be more practical than yours is, however, Mr. Xi. China will remain a most favored nation, and my family, especially my daughter, Ivanka, and her husband, Jared, have just been given special permission to sell their brands to the fantastic Chinese people. We want to personally thank you, President Xi, for your gracious business hospitality, and we know you'll also keep that little tyrant Kim Jung-un in check. Who knows? Maybe you can make him see the light of Capitalism so that our products can one day even be sold over there. It is my honest belief that Communism can always be defeated by giving the people free choice. I mean, what's greater, folks? The best products money can buy or starvation and poverty?"

"I hope I can digest this meal after that speech," I say, and I pick-up a pair of chopsticks, lift the rice bowl to my chin, and start shoveling like a pro. My mother made a point of taking me out to all kinds of ethnic restaurants.

Peng Liyuan, the Chinese President's wife, to my left, turns toward me and smiles. Her eyes watch closely how I eat the fried rice in my bowl. "Most people in your country do not shovel rice with chopsticks. They pick-up like this."

She thrusts her sticks down into the rice bowl and tries to grasp a few grains with the tips.

"Best product may be chopstick. Five thousand years ago, we invent these because we have no fuel in China. Cut everything into small pieces to cook faster in wok. Eat small, keep small appetite, and use sticks for fuel after eating!"

I see that the Maître'd, Pedro, is pushing in a large silver cart with the Peking duck on it. The mysterious disappearance of the hotel staff has forced him into this hard labor. There's a pained expression on his face, and when one of the front wheels suddenly turns right, the cart tips over, and the entire hot duck goes flying across the carpet. It stops just under Sean Spicer's chair.

Not missing a beat, Secretary of State Tillerson says, "Hey, Spicey can't have all of that duck! Save some for us."

Everybody at the table laughs.

"It must be the Valkyries at work," Louise Linton whispers to me.

After the meal is over, I realize I'm alone in the dining room, pouring over my emails. My mother writes, "Break a leg, Nicky! You're my Nick

Carraway."

I'm going to wander into the gilded living room. Everybody else has left the dining room to go there. This is where everybody's supposed to congregate to discuss the play and get some after dinner desert of the famous missile chocolate cake.

Last year, when President Xi Jinping was here, President Trump handed his guest a piece of chocolate cake and told him he had just given the order to launch 59 Tomahawk missiles on President Assad's Air Force in retaliation for Assad's chemical bombing of his own people.

In the foyer before the entrance to the living room, I can see two figures close together. One is a tall male, and the other is a shapely female in a tangerine gown. As I come up to the shadows of the interior, I can see who they are.

Rick Perry and the First Lady, Melania Trump! I am going to hide around this corner so they can't see me, but I'll be able to hear their conversation. My extra-sensory microphone should pick up what they say.

"Rick, I have to see about the staff. I was planning to do a special tribute to George Orwell's *Animal Farm*, but now I have no staff to arrange the pigs and the horse. I told Pedro to take them out into the terrace garden. I'll meet you in your room later."

"Okay, babe. Anita will be playing a round of golf with Trump's party, so that should give us more than enough time to play around on our own."

So, the First Lady is having an affair with the Secretary of Energy. I suppose that's an appropriate department for that kind of energetic exploration.

I simply nod to them as I walk past to enter the lavish Mar-a-Lago Living Room. They don't seem phased one bit. They look as innocent as two contented cattle on Rick's Texas ranch.

CHAPTER THREE: THE LIVING ROOM

This is no living room most Americans would recognize. In fact, as I recall, the American funeral industry changed the name from parlor to living room, in the 1930s, when the laws were written to make it illegal for families to hold funerals at home. The housing developers needed a quick way to get rid of the direct association with death that the term parlor had given.

Today, when we think of parlor, we think of a private funeral parlor where the family goes to view the body and not the main room inside our house. In any case, this living room is so huge and audaciously grand that it could never be confused with death or dying.

Its façade is centered by a large arched glass window, while an entrance drive lined with Washingtonian palms deposits guests beneath a side-elevation *porte cochere*. Clad with Genovese Dorian stone enriched by Barwig-carved sculptures and reliefs, the sheltered entry's steps lead through an elaborated arch surrounding a wrought-iron grille glass door. It opens into the entrance hall's prismatic flourish of geometric niches covered with centuries-old Havemeyer tiles and embellished with Spanish lanterns, marble busts and coats of arms.

Paneled double doors adorned with carved cherubs open into the living room ringed by archways interrupted by Venetian silk needlework panels and crowned by an adaptation of the Thousand Wing Ceiling found at Venice's *Gallerie dell'Accademia*.

It's quite odd seeing all these dignitaries lounging on the antique couches, chairs and loveseats that cover the oriental rugs in the living room. Tall, standing lamps and antique fringed table lamps seem superfluous after you look up and see the two gigantic crystal chandeliers suspended from the twenty-one feet high, gold-leaf ceiling.

All of this grandeur is a bit too much for me, so I look for somebody I know. With her fiancée sitting with a klatch of other cabinet members drinking after-dinner coffees, I see actress Louise Linton sitting with Peng Liyuan and Candy Carson.

There is a string quartet of classical musicians playing chamber selections, mostly Beethoven, on two violins, a viola and a cello. They are in front of the grand piano, and the soft sounds drift our way, making it a pleasurable experience.

"Well, ladies, now you can be part of my media exposé. I plan to find out how the angels from the ceiling have been able to come down to earth. Where, pray tell, do you hide your wings?"

Candy Carson laughs, a full-throated, womanly burst of joyful abandon. She is wearing a dark brown, sequined evening gown that fits her plus size frame very well. "And how much wine did you have at dinner?" She asks me.

"My husband is a surgeon and not an ophthalmologist. But anybody can tell you need your eyes examined."

"I think he means Valkyrie and not angel. We choose who's going to die and go to Valhalla. Speaking of which, I was chosen to play a sonata for our after-dinner enjoyment. If you'll excuse me." Louise stands up and brushes down her evening gown. She smiles, surveys her audience, and slowly walks over to the grand piano. This is the signal for the quartet to stop, and they do so. The blonde actress slides across the bench and looks out at the dignitaries who have now turned to observe her.

Steve Mnuchin, her fiancée, steps away from his group and walks over to stand in front of the piano. He doesn't look like a leading man. He has the clerical look of an accountant for a hedge fund. "Excuse me. Ladies and gentlemen. My fiancée, Louise Linton, will soon be starring in a re-casting of *The Terminator*, because our president's friend from California, Governor Arnold Schwarzenegger, doesn't seem to have the same appeal he once had. So, now folks, she's back! The Scottish Terminator. She is my passion, and she'll be playing Beethoven's *Appassionata III*."

As the music plays, I look over at the two secretaries to President Xi Jinping and his wife. They are really getting it on inside a loveseat. I suppose it must be quite romantic to them to be visiting a strange country and enjoying its opulence.

Behind these two, Jeff Sessions' wife, Mary Blackshear, is sitting alone, staring at the two young people in front of her. Suddenly, as if she is struck by some inner demon, she bends over and picks up an antique Italian vase from the coffee table in front of the couch she is on.

She stands, screams, and runs toward one of the coat of arms hanging on the wall. Mrs. Sessions' hands bring the vase behind her graying head, and she flings it forward. It smashes against the coat of arms and bursts apart, sending shards of expensive porcelain outward like an exploding meteor.

Candy Carson hears the crash and says, "One of the Valkyries?"

Pedro, who is carrying a tray of chocolate cake pieces, says, "No. I think it's Kabbalah. A lot of Jews in here, you know. My staff has disappeared."

Kellyanne Conway is standing next to Dr. Ben Carson. The short blonde with the alternate facts grabs Carson's head in her two hands, and she kisses him with passion.

"Ben, you saved my life! Thank you."

After Kellyanne has walked away, Dr. Tom Price comes up to Ben Carson. "Hey, what was that all about, Ben? I thought you said there was no hope for her cancer."

"Unfortunately, none. In three months she'll be completely bald," Dr. Carson says.

Peng Liyuan, overhears the doctors' conversation. She pulls from her purse two chicken feet and some white feathers. She rubs them across her forehead and then plunges them back inside her purse.

President Trump walks around the room and sees that the group is getting restless. "Well, folks, I know you have important meetings in the morning. We'll have your cars brought around."

As all the guests begin to gather their belongings and move toward the exit, Dick DeVos, the Secretary of Education's husband and founder of Amway, suddenly lays down on one of the couches and falls asleep. Betsy sits down next to him, pulls her feet up on the couch under her gown, and rests her head on his stomach.

Slowly, one by one, each of the guests begins to loosen his or her clothing, yawns, and settles down into a chair, upon a couch and even down on the floor's rug.

"My wife's shawl is missing," Rick Perry says, and he goes into the foyer where I can see Melania Trump waiting for him.

I step gingerly over to the wall next to the foyer to record their conversation once more.

"Why hasn't anybody left yet? It's almost two in the morning. Nobody wanted to play golf, either. We won't have time together, my lover."

"They should be leaving any minute now. You can come up to my bedroom while Donald is saying the good-byes. If he comes in while we're up there, I'll tell him I was showing you the incunabula."

However, I see that nobody is leaving, and President Trump tells them, "I'll have your rooms made-up, my friends. You can stay the night."

None of the guests moves. I can see they are all beginning to caress each other in a strange exhibition of sexual eagerness. In fact, the young Chinese secretaries are actually getting it on beneath a tiger rug near the fireplace. It's as if I'm at a teenage sleepover.

I'm going to snooze right here on this leather couch. I used to sleep on the couch a lot at home. The TV was usually talking to me, but I could always fall asleep to media. This escapade is getting too strange for this sleepy reporter to understand.

CHAPTER FOUR: MY SECRET COUSIN

In the morning, I awaken to the voice of my leader, President Trump. He and Melania chose to sleep in the gilded Living Room and not in their private suite. Mr. Trump's famous pompadour looks a bit disheveled, but his tuxedo is still without wrinkles. He is speaking to Melania next to the grand piano.

"What else can we do? We have to offer them breakfast, right?" Trump tells her.

"I'm sure they'll go home after that," Melania responds, running her hand through a tangle of unruly brown hair. Now that the staff has disappeared, her Israeli hair stylist has also flown the coop.

"I had the most horrid dream!" Education Secretary Betsy DeVos says, rubbing her eyes and glancing down at her husband, Dick, whose head is still on her lap. "We were going to a school choice convention on a train. There was a terrible grinding noise, and then our car was thrust forward until I found myself on the floor of my first-class sleeper. A car filled with poor Amish had been hit by a speeding truck at a crossing. When I saw all the bloody bodies of children and the beards of the men tangled together in a gruesome pile on the tracks, I felt no pity for them. I kept thinking about what a stupid religion they had that forced them to drive horse carriages but permitted them to ride trains. However, when I heard about Princess Diana dying in that limo crash in Paris, many years ago, all I could think about was what a terrible waste of beauty and royalty."

"I think the poor are less sensitive to pain," says Anita Thigpen Perry. "Have you ever seen a wounded bull? Well, I have, out on our ranch. Not a trace of emotion."

I wonder how she can compare animals to people, but then I remember how they've done studies about how readers fail to react to pictures of humans being blown-apart by terrorists as opposed to being shown a photo of some mangy dog being mistreated. The mistreated dog will always be the more sympathetic picture. Somehow, so it seems, humans deserve what they get. Fox News would never let me say this, and the *National Enquirer* will probably edit it also.

When Betsy DeVos tries to wake-up her husband, Dick, he doesn't move.

President Trump sees this and walks over to their couch. "Betsy, why don't we let him rest in one of the bedrooms upstairs?"

Dr. Ben Carson is standing next to Dr. Tom Price. Dr. Price says, "What do you think about Dick's condition, Ben?"

Dr. Carson tugs at his chin. "Within a few hours, he'll be completely bald. I mean, he has just a few hours to live."

Kellyanne Conway, standing nearby, overhears them. "I'm not feeling well myself," she says, and she sits down in an antique chair.

Melania Trump walks over to Pedro, the only staff member remaining. "Pedro, please get breakfast for our guests."

"I'm sorry, Madam, but that's impossible. The groceries haven't been delivered yet." Pedro looks harried and worn down.

"All right then. Bring out some of the dinner from last night."

"Yes, Madam. I've left a cart over in the corner of the Living Room."

"Thank you," Melania says, and she looks over at Rick Perry, who is just rising from his night's sleep next to his wife. Obviously, there was no secret tryst between the two lovers.

General Mattis marches to the center of the sleeping arrangements, and comes to attention, as if he were calling roll on the parade grounds. "I've been watching all of you. Not one of you has been able to leave this room. I think we're all psychologically trapped here. I don't want to cast any stones, but the Communist Chinese used psychological warfare on captured American prisoners during the Korean War. What about it, President Xi? Are you keeping us here by some Manchurian Candidate means?"

A few of the guests laugh. President Xi Jinping strides over to General Mattis and looks him straight in the eye. "No, but perhaps your leader knows why we're not leaving. After all, he's the one who called us all here."

Candy Carson, Kellyanne Conway and Anita Perry walk toward the foyer to exit, probably wanting to clean-up.

Peng Liyuan is watching them leave. She is sitting on a chair next to my divan. She points at them and says, "I'd wager they don't leave." I keep looking at those chicken feet and white feathers sticking out of her purse.

General Mattis seems invigorated by what the Chinese President's wife says. "After last night's party in this room, none of us made the slightest effort to go home. Why is that? Was it normal for us to spend the night together? I saw you, groping at each other in the dark. You were violating the most basic precepts of good etiquette. This room was like a gypsy campground."

President Xi says, "Come now, General. No need to blow things so out of proportion. We were under the spell of the lovely music, the fine food, and the convivial conversation. It was all good cheer. Nothing surprising about this, is there?"

"Melania. Why are you having Pedro serve breakfast in the Living Room rather than in the Dining Room?" President Trump asks.

"I don't really know," says Melania.

"I'm sorry, but I need to see my children off to school," says Kellyanne. "Let's go, George." She gets up, and her corporate attorney husband follows her toward the foyer exit. However, Pedro is wheeling the cart of food over, and they both are pushed back into the main room.

All the guests begin to circle the breakfast cart. Their arms quickly reach out to snatch bread, and they then lift slices of Peking duck and make sandwiches.

"Pedro, please get more spoons from the Dining Room," Melania tells the Maître 'd.

Pedro walks toward the foyer opening, but he stops, reaching for his head as if he were having a migraine attack. He sits down on a chair next to the foyer. His face is pale, and he looks quite ill.

The evening finally arrives, and nobody has left the Living Room. Dick DeVos has gotten worse and has slipped into a comatose state.

I decide something must be done to break this lethargy. The man is dying, and two of them have cancer, probably, so my thoughts turn to an absurd reasoning. If my theory about my not being an accepted member of these wealthy elite is true, then if I approach one of them and prove I am not one of them, then I will be able to leave.

I walk over to my secret cousin, Jared Kushner, who is comforting his lovely wife, Ivanka. They are standing near the black metal grating that covers a door to the outside. Looking like Cinderella and the Prince who can't leave the Ball, they both turn to face me when they hear me approach.

I keep seeing my mother's photo of my great-grandfather as I look at this thirty-five-year-old Orthodox Jew's face. The same dimples in both cheeks and one in his pointed chin. His straight, non-Semitic hair. He is the exact image of Yossel Kushner, Holocaust Survivor, and rail-thin patriarch of the Kushner family.

"Excuse me, Mr. Kushner. My name's Nick Holcomb. I'm a journalist who just so happens to be a cousin of yours. My great-grandmother was the head housekeeper of Charles Munn's Palm Beach Amado mansion. She met our great-grandfather, Yossel, in Florida, shortly after the war. He impregnated my great-grandmother, out of marriage, so that makes us cousins, if my biology is correct."

I expect Kushner to quickly rebuff me, but instead, his face takes on an amused aspect, and he smiles benignly at me. "Ah, yes. Joseph, or Yossel as you call him, was quite the cad. The joke in our family is that our roots began growing in a weed garden and not in Paradise. Was your great-grandmother Irish, by any chance?"

"Why, yes, she was. McKenzie. How did you know?"

"Joe, so the story goes, was always picked-on by the Irish construction workers when he settled with his wife Rae in New York after the war. When my great-grandfather became wealthy from his housing development and investments, it became a game with him to make love to every Irish woman he could find. We must have gone through twenty or more Irish maids and cleaning women in our home. They would become pregnant or the family would pay them to leave after we discovered what Joe was doing. I guess in the case of your great-grandmother, Joe was beginning to wander off the reservation, so to speak."

When he began to laugh in my face, I was livid.

"What makes you any better than other Americans? How dare you to think your relative is an innocent stallion who can plow with anybody he chooses! My great-grandmother suffered greatly by having a bastard daughter. She was a Catholic. They wouldn't even give her a burial mass in the Church! She was an alcoholic who forced my grandmother to pretend to be her sister when they went out dancing together. Your family is the cause of it all. All of you can go straight to hell! I don't belong here reporting about your filthy greed and lust. You're all the ones who are the castaways, not me!"

I turn from them, and I begin to run. I am heading toward the foyer, expecting to dart through the dark hall, down the stairs, and out into the night. I can hear Jared shouting at me, "Wait! Mr. Holcomb! You haven't heard the whole story."

As I cross the entrance to the foyer, I breathe a sigh of relief. At last! I'm free! However, when I try to pass on through to the other side of the foyer, to escape, I stop. Standing there in the darkness, I look back toward the gilded Living Room. The wealthy dignitaries are walking across the floor, under the chandelier lights, like lost souls, and I am reminded of Plato's story of the Cave. Are they real, or are they just the reflections of the fire in our minds? I can't leave them yet. I need to stay here to find out what happens to them. If they are in Hell, then I must be in Purgatory. Kushner said his family grew up in a garden of weeds, so I must stay and see what happens to those who don't keep the promises made in Paradise.

CHAPTER FIVE: REMAIN CALM

I don't know how many hours have passed. At least 24. Not one person in the Trump group has left. I watch Pedro bring what's left of the duck up to his nose. He makes a face and throws it in a trash receptacle next to the serving table. The water is almost gone. Unable to get to any of the lavatories, the guests are using other trash cans that have been strategically located in the corners of the room away from the couches and other furniture. The faces that these erudite folks make as they hike up their gowns and pull down their tuxedo trousers to shit in the trash, would have instantly made the satirical rounds on Trevor Noah's *The Daily Show* and *Full Frontal with Samantha Bee* had this not been such an actual tragedy.

President Trump keeps pacing up and down on the oriental rugs. "I just don't get it. There's got to be a logical solution. We haven't all gone crazy, have we?"

As if on cue, Mrs. Sessions begins to scream again.

"I think it's the staff. Why did they all leave at once?" Reince Priebus says, looking over at Pedro.

"Yeah, like rats leaving a sinking ship," says his wife, Sally.

Pedro is angry. "Excuse me, but my staff didn't know why they were leaving. An hour before you all arrived, they were fine."

President Trump waves his arms in exasperation. "Hey, now, listen. We've got to keep our heads. We're not under some magic spell here. There's got to be a rational explanation for our inability to leave this room. We're not in some haunted mansion."

"The Curse of Post Toasties!" Renda St. Clair, Rex Tillerson's wife giggles.

"How old are you?" Karen Pence asks.

"Sorry, Mr. President, but it was you and your wife who invited us here. Perhaps we should begin our inquisition with both of you." Stephen Bannon, perhaps still stinging from his demotion in the White House, now begins to turn against the hand that feeds him.

Melania walks over to Bannon and slaps him hard on the face. "How dare you! Ingrate! If anybody is causing a disturbance, it's you and your band of anti-Semites. There are riots in Berkeley because of you."

Dick DeVos, dying in his wife's lap, whispers hoarsely, "I'm glad I won't be seeing the extermination."

As if he were able to prophesy his own demise, Dick DeVos passes away that night. Betsy and Pedro take Dick's body and place it inside a large cupboard behind the serving table.

Later, I can see the hand of Dick DeVos fall out of the cupboard door, which had not been secured. Betty Price, resting nearby, sees the hand, screams once, and faints.

I can hear sirens. The police, Secret Service and military have arrived, and their blue, red and white lights flash all around our mansion. My cell phone is vibrating!

"Hello," I say.

"This is James Comey, FBI Director. Are you Nick Holcomb?"

"Y ... y ... yes," I stammer.

"Is everything all right in there? We were given a direct order from President Trump to not intrude on this meeting until he gives us the order. However, we can't connect with POTUS. Can you connect us with him?"

"I'm afraid not. You see, I myself can't leave Mar-a-Lago, nor can I get into the main Living Room where all the officials are right now."

"Why? Who or what's stopping you? Are you all being held hostage?"

"Not exactly. We all seem to be trapped inside this mansion for no apparent reason. Nobody seems to have the will power to exit."

"What do you mean no apparent reason? There's a reason for everything, young man. You're being absurd."

"Then why can't you communicate with President Trump? What's the reason?"

"Well, we don't know yet. It could be a Russian hack. Or, maybe it's a coup. I don't know. But until I get word directly from POTUS, I can't make a move to go inside. Therefore, I suggest you crash their party and put me in touch with the President!"

"I'll do what I can, sir. But, honestly, I can't promise anything." The world outside obviously doesn't have any idea about what's happening in this world.

After four days, the men in the gilded Living Room have gotten desperate. They have taken one of the axes from the wall. Pedro is wielding it, as he knows where the water pipes are inside the walls. I can hear it smash against the plaster and wood. After fifteen or so hefty strokes, Pedro reaches the piping.

"Wait! I'll get some cups!" says Sean Spicer, and he walks over to the serving table, picks up two coffee cups, and returns to the scene of the water excavation.

"Okay, let loose on those pipes," says President Trump, and Pedro cracks into the pipe. A burst of water comes spurting forth, and Spicer quickly fills the cups with precious liquid.

Everybody gets a drink. I lick my dry lips as I watch them.

Later that night, I am curled on the rug inside the foyer trying to sleep. I am too famished and thirsty to do anything but hallucinate. I lift my head to see a tall dark shape looming in front of my entrance. Does he have a grenade? Is he an ISIS member with a beard?

"Psst! Nick. Stand up. I have some water for you." As I stand, my knees begin to buckle, but I keep my frame upright at the mere prospect of a drink of water.

Miraculously, the hand holding the cup of water can break the invisible shield barring me from the Living Room. How is this happening?

"Go ahead. Take it and drink," the voice says.

I gulp it down in three swallows. But, when I attempt to return the cup to the hand, the person has disappeared. I am in a state of panic. If this body could penetrate the foyer, then why couldn't he leave the mansion? No, he chose not to do it. Instead, he was simply giving me a drink of water. A random act of kindness.

I begin to shout out into the Living Room. "Hey! Bring me President Trump! He must talk to Director Comey on my cell phone. They can't enter unless the President tells them directly to do so."

Tragically, nobody seems to be listening to me. Maybe they can't even hear me.

I can do nothing but watch the drama unfolding in the light of the Living Room. The guests are becoming quarrelsome. Peng Liyuan is screaming. She seems to be looking behind the couch at something on the floor.

President Xi walks over to her and they discuss something in Mandarin. President Trump goes over to find out what is happening.

Peng Liyuan tells him, "Our secretaries have killed themselves. They were secret lovers, it seems, and they left a note explaining their disgrace."

"What? Why would lovers kill themselves?" Trump is confused.

"They were blood brother and sister. Both of the Wang family. They believe their incest caused the curse on all of us in this room." Peng Liyuan begins to sob.

"Oh, my God! Incest. That explains it," says President Trump, but I see his eyes as they look over to his daughter, Ivanka, who is standing next to her husband.

"Please! Remain calm. My family spoke about how desperate one can be when trapped inside a concentration camp." Jared steps forth to speak to the group. I then realize who it was who passed me water in the night.

"You! You fucking Jew bastard! I heard you last night as you tried to molest the women in their sleep. You're all alike. Spawn of the Devil!" Stephen Bannon confronts Jared, and they are toe-to-toe on the oriental rug.

Candy Carson begins to cry.

"Shut up, nigger! You smell like a hyena!" Jeff Sessions is shouting at the black woman.

Mrs. Sessions steps forward. "Please, I apologize for my husband. Everything I've most hated since I was a child in Alabama—rudeness, violence, filth—and now that we're inseparable companions, death is preferable to this anarchy! Stop this at once!"

Kellyanne Conway's fever is increasing, and she begins to hallucinate. She gets up from the sofa, grabs her husband George by his arms and begins to dance with him all around the floor. "I am Beauty, and this is my Beast! He has saved me from this madness, and I am alive again. Whatever I say is the truth, and because I say it, it becomes real!"

When Kellyanne begins to choke George, and he starts to gag, Pedro and Jared wrestle her away from him. "Should we tie her hands up?" Pedro asks. "She's delirious."

Jared brings out a handkerchief from his tuxedo jacket, and he ties Kellyanne's hands together. Her husband massages his throat.

Later that night, I wake up to a woman's screams. The actress, Louise Linton, is sitting up on her couch, her breasts exposed. "Somebody was molesting me!" she shouts.

Stephen Bannon immediately rushes at Jared Kushner, grabs him by the throat, and shouts, "You succubus! It's you! You're trying to rape all our women!"

President Trump acts at once. "Stop this at once! I want all the women to sleep on one side of the room, and the men on the other."

Everybody does this, and quiet returns momentarily, except for the starvation that has overtaken the group.

The next morning, I get another call from Comey. "Any luck? It's a media circus out here, Holcomb. All the families of those inside, members from the Chinese Embassy, and every television channel on the planet is out here. You have to get in touch with Trump. Now!"

"Look, don't you think I would have if I could? These people are starving in here. You must get us some food. That wouldn't violate the Instructions of the President, now would it?"

"Yes, it would. No entry, under any circumstances, is the standing order from POTUS. He has his reasons, and he is the final authority under law."

"Then you can't hold me responsible for what happens in here" I say, and I cut him off.

I can hear the squeals as the pigs come up the stairs. I can feel their pink skin as it brushes against my legs in the foyer. Outside, in the Living Room, it is complete chaos. Peng Liyuan has stripped down and is wearing a red table cloth around her naked body, and the chicken feet are attached to either side of her head as she prances around the room. When the three pigs enter, she throws the white feathers at them. "My magic works! We are saved at last!" She screams, and she tackles one of the smaller pigs.

Several of them begin to hack-up furniture, precious antiques, and throw the wood into a pile in the middle of the room. Pedro then turns his axe on the pigs, and blood spews from the neck of each pig as it is attacked. Order seems to be restored in Orwell's world, and President Trump ignites the *Wall Street Journal* with his lighter, and the antiques begin to flame. In twenty minutes, I can smell the tantalizing odor of cooked pork as it wafts over to my foyer Purgatory.

Dark smoke from the primitive fire curls up into the room's wide expanses, past the antique chandeliers, and up into the unreachable air of the angels and their thousand wings.

General "Mad Dog" Mattis has joined with Bannon and George Conway. Kellyanne has died, and the group of men are enraged at Trump. The horse, which has recently entered the room, is now being ridden by Mattis. The Defense Secretary rides the horse up to President Trump. Mattis dismounts. He grabs the President in a hammer lock, and Mattis twists Trump's hands behind his Commander-in-Chief's back.

"You must be sacrificed, Mr. President. Remember President Truman and the Korean War? The buck stops here! When we eat you, everything will return to normal."

The men push Trump toward the fire, but Jared Kushner, Reince Priebus and Rex Tillerson intervene. "Consider the terrible consequences of your actions," says Tillerson. "This vile act of aggression doesn't stand alone. It means the end of human dignity and the reversion to savage beasts!"

"Why can't you have a duel like gentlemen? Like Hamilton and Burr." Sean Spicer shouts.

President Trump breaks free as the men fight and runs over to the serving table. He opens a drawer, pulls out a pistol, and holds it to his head. "There's no need for violence! No use fighting over something so easily achieved. I'm no Jesus Christ, for God sakes!"

Melania rushes over to her husband and grabs the hand with the pistol in it. "Wait! I've been having an affair with Rick Perry. How long have we been here? I don't know. I've lost track. But think how many times each of us has changed places. It's been a horrible eternity, I know, but we've been like pieces on a chess board. We've moved thousands of times. Even the furniture. We've moved it around at least a hundred times. But, look now. Right now. The People and the furniture that's left are exactly where we were that night. Or, am I hallucinating?"

Everybody in the room begins to nod in agreement with her. They are in the same places they were on that first night.

"Louise, go and play that same sonata you played on the first night. But, play just the ending." Melania points toward the grand piano.

We all watch, in rapt suspense, as the blonde actress walks slowly up to the piano bench, sits down, and begins to play the ending to Beethoven's *Appassionata III*.

The guests, in an absurd pantomime, begin talking to each other using the same words they used on that first night. When they begin discussing going home, they realize, with slow amazement, that they can leave the room! As they pass by me in my foyer, they clutch at me, tears of joy streaming down their cheeks.

Behind us, coming up the stairs, are all the relatives, dignitaries, Secret

Service, local police and James Comey. At the end of the parade, my mother, Mandy McKenzie-Holcomb, is standing there, her arms outstretched toward me. "My boy. Nick Carraway. I see you made it."

CHAPTER ZERO: THE NEXT DAY

The next day, at the West Palm Beach Episcopal Church-by-the-Sea, all of us who have survived the Mar-a-Lago incident are here to give thanks. The three pastors of the church preside over the ceremony.

I keep thinking about all the speculation going on in the media. I find it quite interesting that I, who has the truth about what happened, am being completely ignored by the pundits. They find it much more profitable making up all kinds of conspiracy theories of their own. It's a "Kushner Coup," or a "Bannon Rebellion," or a "Chinese Brainwashing Cult," on and on, ad infinitum.

As I sit in this uncomfortable pew seat, next to Jared Kushner, with my mother Mandy on the other side, the President's chief adviser turns toward me and smiles.

"You didn't let me finish my story," he says, referring to what he was going to tell me when I ran away to the foyer.

"Yes, by all means," I say. "Let me hear it."

"Our great-grandfather, Joseph Kushner, was kept prisoner with his wife, Rae, inside an Italian Displaced Persons camp, which was only slightly better than a Nazi concentration camp. You see, Mr. Holcomb, nobody wanted my family because they were not welcome, just as the Syrians are not welcome, and many other victims of war and aggression are not welcome. Even though Joe had a sister in America, he could not get a visa until the Displaced Persons Act was finally passed in 1948 by Congress. My grandmother had seen her Novogrudek ghetto cleansed by the Nazis from 300,000 Jews down to 350."

"My God," I say. "I'm so sorry for you. I mean, for us." I at once began to believe I was being welcomed into the Kushner fold, despite my misgivings of before. It may not be a monetary advantage, but I really don't care about that. It is the dignity of being part of humanity that means something to me and to my mother.

Jared continues, "The only way Rae, my great-grandmother, her father, and her younger sister managed to survive was by escaping from the ghetto in 1943 through a hand-dug tunnel—one through which all the remaining Jews attempted to crawl to freedom. Many didn't survive once they made it to the other side, but, miraculously, Rae, her father, and her sister did—and they were eventually rescued by the legendary Jewish partisan Tuvia Bielski. For a year, they lived in the forest with Bielski's brigade of more than 1,000 Jews until, in the spring of 1944, he brought my family out from the woods. Novogrudek had been liberated by the Soviets."

"I'm sorry, but with that kind of survival instinct, how did your father, Charles, became so embroiled in such political problems?" I ask.

"My father, like our President, is only human. Our great-grandfather,

Joseph, was angry at the Irish and he hated the Roosevelt Administration because he saw them as the reason he and his wife were kept in an Italian DP camp for those years after the war. I guess my father was also angry at the Democrats in power who kept him from doing his business. He saw them as the perpetrators of tax laws and regulations that caused him to lose money. Of course, there is no good reason for breaking the law, so Charles Kushner had to pay for his sins, just as we all must pay. I hope in my current position, I can make amends in some way for my family's actions, but I also want the world to understand that the Kushners will never condone the persecution of immigrants who try to escape war and terror through no fault of their own."

"Yes, I can see now. I am glad you told me," I say, and I take a card he hands me.

"Please. Give me a call. I might be able to help you, Cousin," Jared smiles, and his dimples give me a strangely absurd kind of hope.

After service has ended, we begin to leave the pews and walk down the aisles toward the exit. One of the pastors says, "Why don't we wait until all of the faithful have left?"

Something has happened again. Nobody, including the church-goers, can leave this church.

After an hour, when we still haven't left, I can hear the gunshots outside. A riot. We're all trapped again.

ABOUT THE AUTHOR

James Musgrave's work has been recently featured in *Best New Writing 2011*, Eric Hoffer Book Awards, Hopewell Press, Titusville, N.J. He was semi-finalist in the Black River Chapbook Competition, Fall, 2012. He was also in a Bram Stoker Award Finalist volume of horror fiction, *Beneath the Surface, 13 Shocking Tales of Terror*, Shroud Publishing, San Francisco, CA. His historical mystery series starring Detective Patrick James O'Malley was selected as "featured titles" by the American Library Association's Self-E Program for Independent Authors. The first mystery in that series, *Forevermore*, won the First-Place blue ribbon for Best Historical Mystery, in the Chanticleer International Clue Book Awards, 2013. James lives in San Diego, and is the publisher of EMRE Publishing, LLC.

Sign-up for the Author's Newsletter at emrepublishing.com